Classical Music
Trivia

"*Classical Music Trivia* is a sheer delight to read and will attract the interest of both the musical novice as well as the informed musical professional. The book is not only educational and informative, but real fun. *Classical Music Trivia* is an invaluable aid to anyone wishing to fine-tune their knowledge about classical music."

Lance Bowling, Cambria Master Recordings

Classical Music
Trivia

By Lisa M. Huffman

Consultant to the author,
Carolyn L. Quin, Ph.D.

Illustrations by Victor Cano

THE MASTER-PLAYER LIBRARY
Flagstaff, Arizona

Published by arrangement with The Master-Player Library.

All inquiries should be addressed to:
The Master-Player Library
P.O. Box 3044
Flagstaff, AZ 86003-3044

Library of Congress Catalog Card No. 96-77408

First Edition
ISBN 1-877873-08-X (pbk)

PRINTED IN THE UNITED STATES OF AMERICA

Dedication

To my mother, Judith Anne Still,
who works ceaselessly
to further the field of classical music.

And to my husband, Ron, and
my children, Steven and David,
who supported me through
this project.

Contents

PRELUDE

𝕿 his little trivia book was great fun to write, and I hope that it is just as enjoyable for you, the reader, to read. The purpose of this book is, quite simply, to allow you to enjoy classical music from a different perspective—from the inside out. Whether you consider yourself a novice or a well-versed classical music enthusiast, there is something in this book for you.

The world of classical music is bountifully blessed with anecdotes, anomalies, and the like. For that matter, the classical arts of all facets are enlivened with less known (or less obvious) facts, firsts, peculiarities, and anecdotes immersed in history, humor, and lessons for our daily lives. You will certainly be entertained as this book delights you with its twists and turns through the trivia of classical music.

This book is not an attempt to comprehensively address classical music—its history, its personages, and so on—but to extract some of its most interesting and appealing aspects. Rather than a read-through fact book, this book has been put in a question-and-answer format that will prove to be the most entertaining for you. You will enjoy quizzing yourself and others, keeping in mind that the key is not how many questions you can answer correctly, but how much entertainment and education you derive from them.

1

CLASSICAL MUSIC: A GENERAL PERSPECTIVE

"Servant and master am I:
servant of those dead,
and master of those living.
Through my spirit immortals
speak the message that makes
the world weep and laugh,
and wonder and worship...
For I am the instrument of God.
I am Music."

–Author unknown.

Trivia Questions

𝄞 The "Davidsbündler" ("Members of the League of David" or "David's Band") was an imaginary association invented by composer Robert Schumann. Why did he invent this association?

𝄞 Novelist Arthur Conan Doyle's famous detective character, Sherlock Holmes, was a regular concert- and opera-goer. He was also one of the most remarkable instrumentalists who never lived. What instrument did he play so well?

𝄞 The *Parthenia* was a collection of musical works published in approximately 1611 in England as "the first musicke that ever was printed for the Virginalls." Why is this publication significant?

𝄞 Who is the patron saint of music?

𝄞 For what were the Amati family of the 16th century and the Guarneri and Stradivari families of the 17th century famous?

𝄞 What famous English dramatist who died in 1950 at the age of 94 was also a music critic

𝄞 Can you match these quotes on music with
their authors? 7
  a. "[Music is] The only cheap and
     unpunished rapture upon earth."
  b. "After silence, that which comes nearest
     to expressing the inexpressible is music."
  c. "Music, moody food of us that trade in
     love."
  d. "Good music penetrates the ear with
     facility and quits the memory with
     difficulty."
  e. "Unperformed music is like a cake in the
     oven—not fully baked."
                Matches with . . . ?
  1. Sydney Smith, English clergyman (1771-
     1845).
  2. Sir Thomas Beecham, English conductor
     (1879-1961)
  3. William Shakespeare in *Anthony and
     Cleopatra*, c.1606.
  4. Aldous Huxley, English writer (1894-
     1963).
  5. Issac Stern, Russian-born violinist (born
     1920).

♪ Some musical instruments have properties that make them unique. Name the instruments that have these special attributes: 9
   a) An instrument that has colored strings?
   b) An instrument that is played without the performer touching it?
   c) Two instruments that change shape during a performance?
   d) An orchestral instrument that can be carried in the vest pocket?
   e) An instrument that is carried by the player around the waist like a life preserver?

♪ Who was the only professional musician among the signers of the Declaration of Independence? 10

♪ What is the significance of an 11th century French monk and music theorist named Guido d'Arezzo, and the following Latin hymn to Saint John the Baptist as they relate to the field of music?:
   *"**Ut** queant laxis*
   ***Re**sonare fibris*
   ***Mir**a gestorum*
   ***Fa**mili tuorum*
   ***Sol**ve polluti*
   ***La**bii reatum*
   ***S**ancte Johannes!"*

[Loosely translated as "Keep my lips pure, that as thy servant I may sing praises of thy wondrous deeds, Saint John."—Dorothy Waage.]

𝄢 His remark on music in *The Mourning Bride* (1697) has since been shortened and distorted to be commonly quoted as "to soothe the savage beast." What was William Congreve's original remark regarding music?

𝄢 Acclaimed author Oscar Wilde in "Impressions of America" (*Leadville*, 1883) wrote of this sign that he found posted: "Please do not shoot the pianist. He is doing his best." In what environment, was this sign posted?

𝄢 Prior to the introduction of the 33 and 45 rpm long-playing records which allowed for up to 30 minutes of playing time per side, recordings on the existing 78 RPM (10″ disc) records were significantly shorter. Approximately how long was a recording on a 78 RPM record?

𝄢 In Greek mythology, she is the Muse of music and lyric poetry. Her symbol is the flute and some legends say she invented the flute and all wind instruments. Who is she?

𝄞 Can you identify these instruments by their affectionate or informal nicknames?............. 16

a) Slush pump
b) Squeeze box or ram's horn
c) Sweet potato
d) Doghouse or bull fiddle
e) Licorice stick
f) Fish horn
g) The Kitchen

🎼 Thomas Alva Edison, who invented the phonograph in 1877, insightfully expressed "recording of music" as only one of numerous possibilities for the new device. However, it was some time and many improvements before musical recordings could be produced for commercial consumption. What was Edison's first trial statement into his "speaking telegraph" invention, which is sometimes rendered musically?

🎼 Besides having a musical association, how do the following share a "celestial" affliation?:

- Cosima Wagner–illegitimate daughter of Hungarian composer Franz Liszt and second wife of German composer Richard Wagner.
- Dinant–City in southern Belgium identified as the birthplace of Adolphe Sax, inventor of the saxophone.
- Turandot–The daughter of the Emperor of China in Puccini's opera by the same name.
- Composers Brahms, Ryba, Bartók, Grieg, Debussy, Still, Chopin, Smetana, Schubert, Purcell, Pachelbel, Beruti, and others.
- And many, many more.

🎼 *Muzak*, the first company in the United States to to transmit background or "canned" music in public places, such as restaurants and elevators, was founded in 1934 and was originally named "Wired Radio, Inc." What prominent American company's name was used to form the *Muzak* corporate title? 19

𝄞 Many historical figures, known for other pursuits, were also amateur musicians. Can you name the instruments that these well-known American figures play or played? 20
   a) Albert Einstein
   b) Richard Nixon
   c) Benjamin Franklin
   d) Harry Truman
   e) Thomas Jefferson
   f) Bill Clinton

𝄞 "And it came to pass, when the people heard the sound of the _____, and the people shouted with a great shout, that the wall fell down flat." What instrument is reported in the Bible to have brought down the walls of Jericho? 21

𝄞 Shortly after the printing of the famous Gutenburg Bible, the first book with printed musical examples was produced in Gutenburg's workshop in 1457. What was the title of this significant work? 22

𝄞 One of America's earliest publishers of music was established in 1832, in Boston, and conducted business for over a century. Can you name this company? 23

𝄞 Certain countries have pioneered in furthering classical music in various ways:

Where were the first public concerts held? ... 24

Where was the first performing arts society established to protect artists copyrights? 25

Where was the first periodical containing critical evaluations of musical works published?

.... 26

♪ What Greek myth recounts the tale of a godlike singer who could move people, particularly women, and inanimate objects, by his songs?
.... 27

♪ What nation was the first to organize music festivals devoted to classical music performances and to hold the earliest festival devoted to the works of a single composer?.................... 28

♪ In 1945 in Paris, following a ballet performance, the ballerinas fled the stage in tears after American soldiers expressed their appreciation of the performance by energetic whistling. What insult had the military audience unknowingly paid to the performers?......................... 29

♪ The Ricordi firm in Italy maintains an important position in music publishing. How does Ricordi maintain this position? 30

♪ *The New England Psalm Singer*, by William Billings, was published in 1770 and was the first published collection of wholly American music as well as the first tune book produced by a single composer. The collection was comprised largely of vocal music for the church. And, importantly, the front of this publication was engraved by a famous Bostonian and Revolutionary War figure. Who was he? 31

Theodore Pachelbel, son of famed organist and composer Johann Pachelbel, is said to have given New York City its first of these in 1736. What was it?.. 32

Following the death of his dog, an artist named Francis Barraud painted a rendering of his favorite fox terrier as he used to sit inquisitively listening to his phonograph and called the portrait, "His Master's Voice." Later, Barraud altered the portrait to feature a gramophone, instead of a phonograph, and sold it to the small and obscure, Gramophone Company in London. This HMV logo became pivotal in the success of the Gramophone Company, as well as other organizations worldwide who have utilized it in their advertisements through the years. What was the name of the real-life canine music lover? 33

What is the significance of the *Bay Psalm Book* issued in Cambridge, Massachusetts, first in 1640 and again in 1690? 34

It is commonly known that America's national anthem, *The Star-Spangled Banner*, was written by Francis Scott Key while he was briefly imprisoned during the bombardment of Fort McHenry in the War of 1812. However, do you know some of these lesser-known facts about our national anthem?:

𝄞 This small, pitch-keeping gadget was invented by Handel's famed trumpeter, John Shore, in 1711, and proved very useful to musicians and piano-makers until technological advancements rendered it a near-gimmick. What's the gadget?

𝄞 The Covent Garden Opera House in London was the site of the first musical strike in 1766. The strike, initiated by ballet dancers, was attributed to what dissatisfaction?

𝄞 Johannes Tinctoris authored what publication 'first' in music history about 1498?

𝄞 *More on the phonograph . . .*
Who is commonly accepted as the first classical artist to make a phonograph recording?
How many grooves does the average LP record have?
Émile Berliner invented the phonograph disc in 1888. What is the significance of Berliner's recording of "The Lord's Prayer?"
When did the long-playing record (LP) make its public début? The cassette tape? And the compact disc?

𝄞 The New York Philharmonic conducted by Zubin Mehta gave a free open-air concert in

Central Park, New York City to an estimated 800,000 attendees. In what year did this concert achieve record-breaking attendance for a classical audience: 1962, 1979, 1986, or 1989? 45

𝄞 This music teacher invented the laryngoscope, an instrument used to inspect a person's throat, which proved more helpful to the medical community than to the intended music community. Who was this individual? 46

Answers

1   Schumann invented the "Davidsbündler" to expose the Philistines (adversaries) of the musical world. Yet, while the association was imaginary, it boasted the membership of real individuals, such as Schumann, himself, and Mendelssohn.

2   Sir Arthur Conan Doyle's great detective was a violinist of outstanding aptitude.

3   The *Parthenia* is considered to be the earliest book of music printed from engraved plates in England.

4   Though it is not completely understood why, Saint Cecilia (martyred about A.D. 176 in Italy) is said to be the patron saint of music.

5   These families were the leaders in violin making and they were all from Cremona, Italy.

6   The musical critiques of George Bernard Shaw (1856-1950) provided a picture of music in London at the end of the 19th century and are remembered as witty and penetrating. Shaw's use of the pen name "Corno di bassetto" indicates his intent to compare the rarity and

unconventional quality of the bassett horn (or alto clarinet) with his style of writing.

7   Matches: *a* matches *1*, *b* matches *4*, *c* matches *3*, *d* matches *2*, *e* matches *5*.

8   A maker of woodwind instruments at Nuremburg, Denner is said to have "invented" the clarinet about 1700 after having modified and improved a single-reed folk instrument. The clarinet was first used in an orchestra about 1726.

9   The instruments with these unique attributes are:
   a) The harp–C strings are red and F strings are blue.
   b) The Theremin–an electronic instrument that produces notes by variations in the frequency of an oscillating electric circuit, controlled by movement of the player's hand (or hands) in the air towards, or away from, an antenna.
   c) The accordion and the trombone.
   d) The piccolo. It is 12 inches long.
   e) The Sousaphone–a type of tuba produced in the late 1890's specifically for John Philip Sousa's renowned marching band and still used today.

10 Philadelphian Francis Hopkinson (1737-1791) was the only professional musician to sign the Declaration of Independence. He is also the composer of what has been said to be the first published song composed by an American (*My Days Have Been So Wondrous Free*, 1759) and the composer of *The Temple of Minerva* (1781), a piece enjoyed by George Washington.

11 Guido d'Arezzo was probably the first to use syllables to represent the notes of the tetrachord. For the syllables *ut-ré-mi-fa-sol-la-si* (with different syllables having since been developed to represent the notes of the scale in different languages), he used the first syllables of the Latin hymn. Today the solfeggio syllables do-re-mi-fa-sol-la-ti-do represent the intervals of the major scale.

12 William Congreve is credited with saying, "Music hath charms to soothe a savage breast, /To soften rocks, or bend a knotted oak."

13 This sign was posted in an old Western saloon.

14 The duration of a recording on a 78 RPM record (10″ disc) was, on average, three minutes.

15 She is Euterpe, one of nine sister goddesses presiding over song and poetry and the arts and sciences.

16 The instruments with these nicknames are the:
    a) Trombone
    b) Accordion
    c) Ocarino
    d) Double bass
    e) Clarinet
    f) Oboe
    g) Percussion

17 Edison's first trial statement uttered into his new phonograph was purportedly a nursery rhyme: "Mary had a little lamb, its fleece was white as snow, and everywhere that Mary went, her lamb was sure to go." Besides being a bit of Americana, it met the ten-second length limitation for the new device.

18 Besides having a musical association, these all have minor planets (or asteroids) in the solar system named after them.

19 The "Wired Radio, Inc." company hoped to capitalize on the growing success of the Kodak company by borrowing its corporate name to form the new name, Muzak.

20 These amateur musicians played the:
   a) Violin
   b) Piano
   c) Glass harmonica
   d) Piano
   e) Harpsichord, violin, and recorder
   f) Saxophone

21 "... the sound of the *trumpet*..."–In the Book of Joshua (Joshua 6:20), it is related that the Lord instructed Joshua to have seven priests blow seven trumpets in order to destroy the city of Jericho.

22 The first book with printed musical examples was the *Psalterium*.

23 One of America's first music-publishing firms was the Oliver Ditson & Company (originally Parker & Ditson) and was named after its founder, Oliver Ditson (1811-1888).

24 Public concerts were first organized in England, by pioneering John Banister, and then in France, under the guidance of Anne Philidor.

25 The oldest performing arts society is the French *Société des auteurs, compositeurs, et éditeurs de musique* formed in 1851.

26 Germany pioneered in musical journalism, with musical critiques published in the *Allgemeine musikalische Zeitung* from 1798 to 1881.

27 The myth of Orpheus.

28 England founded "The Three Choirs Festival," the first classical music festival, in 1724 which took place in Gloucester, Hereford, and Worcester. The "Handel Festival" was organized in London during 1857.

29 The Parisian dancers took the enthusiastic whistling as an ill-mannered expression of displeasure. Booing might create an equivalent reaction in the United States today.

30 The Ricordi music-publishing firm, established in 1808 and based in Milan, specializes in the publication of operas and handles the rich cache of operas by Bellini, Boito, Catalani, Donizetti, Menotti, Montemezzi, Pizzetti, Poulenc, Puccini, Respighi, Rossini, Verdi, and Zandonai.

31 Paul Revere of Revolutionary War fame engraved the frontispiece of this publication.

32 The younger Pachelbel is credited with giving New York City its first concert in 1736.

33   The real-life dog depicted in the gramophone advertisements was named Nipper.

34   The *Bay Psalm Book* was the first book of music printed in the North American colonies and only the second book published in America. When issued originally in 1640, the publication contained no musical examples, but, it was reissued in 1690 with twelve musical examples.

35   F. S. Key borrowed America's national anthem from *To Anacreon in Heaven*, a song by English organist-composer, John Stafford Smith. Smith, a member of the "Anacreontic Society," wrote it as a theme song for this singing club.

36   Congress passed the bill making *The Star-Spangled Banner* America's national anthem on March 3, 1931.

37   A federal law states that *The Star-Spangled Banner* cannot be played in part or in a manner that transgresses from the standard composition, such as with extracted melodies or embellishments to the music. Igor Stravinsky discovered this law when, after conducting the Boston Symphony Orchestra in January 1944 in an embellished, and not well-received, version

of *The Star-Spangled Banner*, the Bostonian police were sent to preside over Stravinsky's second concert in order to assure that no further infringement of the law took place. Stravinsky, having been forewarned, conducted this and future performances with the standard version of the anthem.

38 The tuning fork.

39 The pampered ballet dancers objected to wearing worsted (coarser, less desirable) stockings instead of the traditional silk.

40 Tinctoris wrote the first dictionary of music, published by Treviso. This dictionary has been considered crucial to current understanding of Renaissance musical practice and theory.

41 Pianist Josef Hofmann (1876-1957), at the age of twelve in 1888, was the first classical artist to make a phonograph recording.

42 One continuous groove.

43 This Berliner recording is thought to be the oldest surviving phonograph recording.

44 1948, 1965, 1983.

45 The record for attendance to a classical concert was set in the year 1986.

46 Manuel Garcia invented this medically-helpful device.

2

OPERA: MUSIC, PERFORMERS, AND PERFORMANCES

𝕿 hroughout history, singing has been the most widespread and common way of making music. It is no wonder that the Baroque development of opera--with the combination of drama, costumes, scenery, poetry, and theatrical expertise--was instantly embraced by audiences. With its local beginnings in Italy, opera now delights the senses of people around the world and will retain a permanent place in the classical arts.

In addition, operatic music and performers of opera have had influences and experiences off-stage that are both unusual and memorable. See how well-versed you are on the extraordinary world of opera in the upcoming pages.

Trivia Questions

♪ Used to describe European classical music from the late 17th century and early 18th century, what is the origin of the word 'baroque'? 1

♪ This individual contributed more than any other music professional to the success of the recording device, having made over 150 records and cyclinders. He is considered the first true "gramophone" tenor. Who is this tenor? Can you name his earliest known recording? 2

♪ Who was the first Afro-American composer to have an opera produced in the United States by a major New York opera company? 3

♪ As a young orphan, this opera performer was often neglected and imprisoned in the home of her widowed and easily-angered care provider. One day, as a six-year-old, she was singing while making hair braids for her care provider to sell at market. An influential lady passing by heard her beautiful voice through an open window and stopped to listen. Discovering the girl's situation from neighbors, this lady eventually got her schooled and admitted as a pupil to the Royal Theatre in Stockholm. A number of years later, she was brought to the United States by P.T. Barnum of circus fame and became known as the "Swedish Nightingale." Who was this orphan girl? 4

♪ What opera was the first composed by an American-born composer to be performed at the famous La Scala Opera House in Milan and who was the composer? 5

♪ French chef Auguste Escoffier created the ice cream dessert he called Pêches Melba and first served it to what Australian opera star after whom he named his creation? A kind of toast is also named after her. 6

♪ Auturo Toscanini described the voice of this contralto as one "that comes once in a hundred years." She was the first Afro-American opera singer to perform at the Metropolitan Opera in New York. What was her name? 7

♪ This acclaimed writer once noted, "But for opera, I could never have written *Leaves of Grass*." Who was he? 8

♪ What Scandinavian opera performer in the 20th century was considered "the greatest Wagnerian soprano of her day?" 9

♪ Beethoven only wrote one opera, despite the many classical works to his credit. It is the most famous of all "rescue operas." Can you name Beethoven's only opera? 10

♪ What three performers were featured at *In Concert* held at the 1990 Soccer World Cup Finals in Rome, Italy? They also have one of the best-selling classical albums of all time. 11

♪ What composer was the first Afro-American to have an opera televised over a national network in the United States (after his death)?............. 12

♪ To whom do we attribute the development of *verisimo* or naturalism, a new style of opera? 13

♪ *Celos aun del ayre matan* was a Spanish opera written by Juan Hidalgo (who died in 1685). Why is this opera significant? 14

♪ Name the opera that was staged 10 weeks before the death of composer Wolfgang Amadeus Mozart? 15

♪ Who is revered as the "Father of German Romantic Opera?" 16

♪ Scott Joplin (1868-1917), who is more generally known for his "ragtime era" compositions, wrote two operas. What are the names of these operas and which of these operas was produced

♪ Lewis Hallam was responsible for establishing this in 1752. What was it? 24

♪ Opera is said to have begun in 1600 with Jacopo Peri's opera, *Eurydice*. Why? 25

♪ Who was the "Father of French Opera?" 26

♪ This opera depicts the marital conflicts of a young couple and features a bathtub aria and a hymn to hot water. Can you name this opera and its composer? 27

♪ This work made operatic history because it was written for an Afro-American cast. Name the opera and its composer. 28

♪ *The Sounds of Time* by Simon Rees and Peter Reynolds was performed by Rhian Owen and Dominic Burns in March 1993 at Hayes, Wales. What record does this opera hold? 29

♪ Ernestine Schumann-Heink took one of her children to see an operatic performance at the Metropolitan Opera in which she played a key role. In the climatic scene, the child began screaming hysterically, "They're killing my Mama!" Based on a Grimm Brothers' fairy tale,

♪ This Italian-born, American composer wrote the first opera to have its world premiere televised. Name the composer and the opera. 36

♪ The Bayreuth opera theater was built for Richard Wagner by King Ludwig II and is dedicated to the works of Wagner. Officially opened in 1882, the theatre was revolutionary in its design. What structural feature enhanced the enjoyment of live opera? 37

♪ Tenor Mario Lanza portrayed Enrico Caruso in the famous movie, *Caruso*. Yet, in spite of being chosen to portray the great Caruso, Lanza is credited with how many fully staged performances during his lifetime? 58

♪ This opera has no human beings cast in its story. What opera is it? 59

♪ What former actress, with the help of her multimillionaire husband, was instrumental in saving the Metropolitan Opera from financial ruin during the Great Depression? She also founded the Metropolitan Opera Guild. 60

♪ Tenor Ezio Pinza appeared in a short-lived television comedy in the 1950's. What show was it? 61

♪ "Don," a distinction generally denoting refinement or stature, is used liberally in the operatic arts for male characters. The "Dons" in operas, such as Don Giovanni, Don Juan, and Don Quixote, are numerous. However, there is one opera in which "Don" is used as a proper name and denotes a female character. Can you name this opera and its creator? 62

♪ In one of Alban Berg's operas, he introduces a military band, an out-of-tune piano, and an accordion. Which opera is it? 63

♪ Name a dance scene from an opera in which a strip-tease takes place? 64

♪ This soprano was an avid baseball fan and, at one time, was part-owner of a major league baseball team. Who was she?....................... 65

♪ Some performers in opera have been known to have unusual superstitions in connection with their stage appearances. Identify the individuals who held the following superstitions:............ 66

   a) This Italian soprano, who achieved her greatest notoriety very early in the 20th century, customarily dropped a dagger to the floor prior to each stage appearance, believing that its landing upright meant a successful performance.

   b) This Austrian soprano, known primarily for her Italian and French coloratura roles between the World Wars, insisted that success on the stage was indicated by getting a glimpse of a chimney sweep prior to a performance. (Her manager went to great lengths to have a chimney sweep make a showing to her before each performance.)

   c) This American mezzo-soprano, who performed largely at the Metropolitan Opera, thought that having a manicure on the day of a performance was bad luck.

♪ What is the actual difference between the High C of a soprano and the High C of a tenor?..... 67

♪ This opera by Gian Carlo Menotti is the first stage work to use an expletive in the text. The story depicts a wife who charges tourists two dollars to view her husband in his record-breaking sleep, and who brings fame to the town. Do you know the name of this Menotti opera? 68

♪ The famed castrato Carlo Farinelli (1705-1782) was engaged by a royal figure to sing for him each night in order to alleviate his chronic melancholy. For 25 years, Farinelli sang the same four songs to him until he died. What royal figure engaged Farinelli's musical talents in this way? 69

♪ Can you name the opera and its composer in which the heroine's secret is that she indulges in cigarette smoking?...................................... 70

♪ The overture of the opera, *Uthal* (1806), by Etienne-Nicolas Méhul (1763-1817), is unique. How is this overture distinguished from that of others?.. 71

♪ In what opera does a mechanical doll sing? .. 72

♪ New York can boast the loudest of its long history of being a center of fine opera in the United States. However, where else in the United States did opera enjoy a significant patronage for a long period? 73

♪ The popular, "barber-shop" style song, *Sweet Adeline*, was written by composers R.H. Gerard (lyrics) and Harry Armstrong (music) in 1903 for what concert and operatic soprano? 74

Answers

1   Taken from the Spanish word, "barrueco," which means a strangely-shaped pearl, the word developed into an indication of something grotesque. Borrowed from the word's first usage in describing architectural style, "baroque" came to mean a highly ornamented style. However, most classical music enthusiasts will say that they find most music from the Baroque period anything but grotesque.

2   Enrico Caruso (1873-1921) achieved great success with his operatic recordings from 1902 to 1920. His earliest known recording is "E lucevan le stelle" from Puccini's *Tosca*.

3   Afro-American composer, William Grant Still (1895-1978) had his opera, *Troubled Island*, produced in 1949 by the New York City Opera. *Troubled Island* is based on the Haitian revolution with libretto written by Langston Hughes.

4   This orphan was Johanna "Jenny" Maria Lind, (1820-1887) whose acclaim in the United States greatly surpassed the limited success she had known in her native Sweden.

5   The folk opera, *Porgy and Bess*, by George

Gershwin (1898-1937) was the first to have a La Scala Opera House audience.

6   The Australian opera star, Nellie Melba (1859-1931), was the first to be served Escoffier's creation: the dessert was called "Peach Melba" and the toast, "Melba Toast." Interestingly, her name was originally Helen Mitchell.

7   Marian Anderson (born 1902) became the first Afro-American to perform at the Metropolitan Opera in 1955 as Ulrica in Verdi's *Un ballo in maschera* (or, *Masked Ball*).

8   This noted writer was Walt Whitman.

9   Kirsten Flagstad (1895-1962) began her career in Norway and began performing in the United States in the 1930's. One of the greatest 20th century dramatic sopranos, Flagstad was a favorite with audiences until her retirement from the stage in 1954.

10   *Fidelio* or *Die Eheliche Liebe* (*Wedded Love*), Op. 72 (1805) is Beethoven's only opera, and is based on a French play by Bouilly called *Leonore*. In Beethoven's opera, the devotion of the main character, *Leonore*, ultimately frees her husband, *Florestan*, from political imprisonment.

11   The performance of José Carreras, Placido Domingo, and Luciano Pavarotti at *In Concert* was considered to be an international success.

12   The first Afro-American to be honored with the televising of one of his operas over a national network was William Grant Still (1895-1978). Still's opera, *A Bayou Legend*, was televised over PBS (Public Broadcasting System) in 1981.

13   Italian composer, Pietro Mascagni (1863-1945), introduced the style of *verismo* and achieved notoriety with his first one-act opera, *Cavalleria Rusticana*. However, because he was used by the pre-World War II Facists as a musical sounding board, Mascagni was boycotted by Italian musicians and ended his years in disgrace.

14   This opera is the earliest Spanish opera to survive (although in part) and was first performed in Madrid in 1660.

15   Mozart's last opera, *The Magic Flute* (1791), was staged just prior to his death.

16   Carl Maria von Weber's (1786-1826) work laid the foundations for German national opera and created a turning point in German musical history.

17 *A Guest of Honor* (of which the score has been lost) and *Treemonisha* are the titles of Joplin's only two operas, and it was *Treemonisha* (1911) which was produced at Joplin's own expense in 1915. Without scenery, costumes, or orchestra, this production proved unsuccessful. Joplin's death two years later is said to have been hastened by the opera's sad failure.

18 The first American female conductor of significance, Sarah Caldwell (born 1924), became the first female conductor at the Metropolitan Opera in 1973.

19 The name of French soprano, Louise Dugazon (1755-1821), became synonymous with a type of French soprano voice in association with a soubrette (a light soprano comedic role). The type of voice was divided into four subcategories: jeune Dugazon, première Dugazon, forte Dugazon, and mère Dugazon.

20 "La Divina" performed under the name of Maria Callas (1923-1977).

21 The Great Caruso (1873-1921) set this one-night box office record.

22 Verdi's opera *Aïda*, which tells of the conflict between love and patriotism in the Egypt of the

Pharaohs, was performed for a Yankee Stadium crowd in 1925.

23 Composer Georg Benda (1722-1795) is credited with the earliest known opera based on the subject of Romeo and Juliet (*Romeo und Julie*, 1776).

24 Lewis Hallam founded America's first opera company, The American Company, in 1752. However, the oldest continuously performing opera company is the Metropolitan Opera Company of New York City, which held its first season in 1883 and still performs today.

25 Peri's *Eurydice* is the oldest surviving opera. Peri's older opera, *Daphne*, composed in 1597, is now lost.

26 Jean-Baptiste Lully (1632-1687), a French composer of Italian origin, established the chief characteristics of French opera.

27 *News of the Day* is the name of this opera by Paul Hindemith (with libretto by Marcellus Schiffer). It was first performed in Berlin in 1929. Other novelties of the opera include its use of a chorus of stenographers at their percussive typewriters.

28 The opera was *Porgy and Bess* by George Gershwin (1898-1937). This was Gershwin's only opera.

29 *The Sounds of Time* holds the record for being the shortest opera ever performed. The performance in Wales lasted for 4 minutes and 9 seconds.

30 The opera was *Hansel and Gretel*, in which Ernestine Schumann-Heink played the witch, whom the principle child characters push into the oven at the end.

31 The sporting events or pastimes featured in these works are:
   a. Bullfighting
   b. Archery
   c. Boxing
   d. Baseball
   e. Chess
   f. Crap-shooting

32 Afro-American tenor, Thomas Bowers (1836-1885).

33 Caterina Jarboro appeared in the title role of Verdi's *Aïda* with the Chicago Opera Company in April 1933.

34 American suffragette, Susan B. Anthony, and the second U. S. President, John Adams, are depicted in this opera.

35 Henry Purcell (1659-1695) is considered to be the first English opera composer, and is known best for his operas, *Dido and Aeneas* and *The Fairy Queen*. The opera, *Dido and Aeneas*, is distinguished for being the oldest opera in English that is still regularly performed.

36 Gian Carlo Menotti's opera, *Amahl and the Night Visitors*, had its television premiere on Christmas Eve, 1951, after having been commissioned by the National Broadcasting Company.

37 The orchestra pit of the theatre was built underneath the stage. This placement turned the pit into a sounding box so that the performers could actually feel the music beneath them. The blended sound, then, of both the performers and the orchestra, projected into the amphitheater.

38 The original libretto of this opera involved the assassination of a European monarch.

39 Soprano Lillian Nordica (1857-1914).

40 Leonard Warren fell dead onstage on March 4, 1960, after suffering a stroke.

41 Robert McFerrin was the first Afro-American male to sing at the Metropolitan Opera.

42 Rosa Ponselle (1897-1981) suffered from chronic stage fright.

43 Di Stefano made some of his first recordings while interned in a POW camp during World War II.

44 Arthur Miller's play, *The Crucible*, about the witchcraft trials of 1692 in Salem, Massachusetts, was adapted by composer Robert Ward. The opera had its first performance in 1961.

45 Joan Sutherland (born 1926).

46 Tenor Luciano Pavarotti has advertised the American Express Card.

47 Opera performer, Ezio Pinza (1892-1957), played the main male role in this film.

48 Milnes (born 1935) sang the Marlboro cigarette jingle, "You get a lot to like with a Marlboro."

49 It is the opening line for Puccini's *La Bohème*, in which the character Marcello jokes to the character Rodolfo that the sea in his painting is

to blame for the intense cold of their attic living space.

50 Parma, Italy, holds the reputation for having the toughest opera audience.

51 Milan's La Scala Opera House always opens its season on December 7th, Pearl Harbor Day.

52 Nilsson (born 1918) exiled herself from the United States from 1975-1979 and listed administrator Sir Rudolph Bing as a "dependent" on her U.S. federal income tax return—she claimed "he needed her."

53 Both soprano Galina Vishnevskaya and conductor Mstislav Rostropovich had defected to the West and had been stripped of their Soviet citizenship.

54 The religious opera, *Dialogues des Carmélites*, by French composer Francis Poulenc (1899-1963), with a libretto by Bernanos, was adapted from the film by the same name.

55 In a New York City subway station.

56 The folk opera, *The Tender Land* (1954).

57 For the coronation of Queen Elizabeth II.

58 Tenor Mario Lanza sang only one fully-staged performance in his life.

59 The operatic characters in *Das Rheingold* are all supernatural.

60 The Metropolitan Opera was saved with the help of Actress Eleanor Robson (or Mrs. August Belmont).

61 Pinza starred as a music-loving widower with a houseful of children in the situation comedy, *Bonino*.

62 The opera is *The Children of Don* (part of a Wagnerian trilogy called the *The Cauldron of Anwyn*) by English composer Joseph Holbrooke (1878-1958). The character Don is the Earth Goddess.

63 *Wozzeck*.

64 The "Dance of the Seven Veils" in Strauss's opera, *Salome*.

65 Soprano Helen Traubel (1899-1972) was the former, part-owner of the St. Louis Browns.

66 The individuals who have held these superstitions are:

    a) Luisa Tetrazzini (1871-1940)
    b) Selma Kurz (1874-1933)
    c) Rose Bampton (born 1909)

67   The High C of a soprano is two octaves above the middle C of the piano, while the tenor's High C in only one octave above.

68   The seventeenth of Menotti's operas, *The Hero* (1976), is the first to use an expletive in the text.

69   King Philip II of Spain.

70   *The Secret of Suzanne* by Ermanno Wolf-Ferrari (1876-1948).

71   It is the only overture to include a part for solo voice in which a soprano sings/utters two declamatory notes at the climax.

72   In Offenbach's *The Tales of Hoffmann*, the mechanical doll sings the "Doll's Song."

73   New Orleans' French Opera House enjoyed a steady patronage for a time in the early history of opera in the United States.

74   Gerard and Armstrong wrote this work with soprano Adelina Patti in mind.

75 Verdi's *Ernani* was released in 1903 by the Italian company, HMV, on forty single-sided discs.

76 *Home Sweet Home* was composed by Sir Henry Bishop, with a libretto by John Howard Payne.

77 She is Japanese soprano, Tamaki Miura (1884-1946).

78 Puccini's *Suor Angelica* consists of an all-female cast.

79 During the 18th and early part of the 19th centuries, it was common practice to have the secondary soprano sing an aria in the second act of an opera. At this time, ices were sold in the audience, and thus, the term "ice cream aria" came about.

3

INSTRUMENTAL AND CHAMBER MUSIC

$\mathfrak{I}$nstrumental and chamber music, by design, are naturally more personal than their grander orchestral companions. But, in spite of smaller resources, the absence of a conductor, and a lighter, more intimate sound, instrumental and chamber music are of immense importance to classical music as a whole, since there are many more chamber recitals than orchestral concerts in any given locale. The pages that follow will test your knowledge of non-orchestral compositions, and of the anecdotes, anomalies and pecularities of instrumental music.

Trivia Questions

𝕴 Who originated the piano "recital" and was the first to give an entire concert without an orchestra or assisting musicians?.................................1

𝕴 What English individual was the first musician-composer to be buried at Westminister Abbey where he had been the principal organist from 1679 until his death in 1695?..........................2

𝕴 He never wrote an opera or an oratorio, nor did he produce a symphony or a string quartet. The keyboard was his chosen medium. Who was this Polish-born composer exiled from his country? 3

𝕴 Frederick the Great (1712-1786), King of Prussia, was a skilled instrumentalist. What instrument did he play, and for what instrument did he compose music?...................................4

𝕴 Why did Italian violinist Giuseppe Tartini (1692-1770) seek refuge with the Franciscan friars at Assisi? 5

𝕴 What classical master had an ear so sensitive that he could perceive when a violin was tuned

What composer is associated with the musical term *bagatelle*, which literally means "trifle?"

King Henry V composed church music under what pen-name?

Clara Wieck, considered to be the greatest female pianist of her generation in 19th century Europe, was married to what famous composer?..9

Who is the first Afro-American to achieve superstar status as a classical pianist?............. 10

After being dismissed from St. Stephen's Cathedral as a chorister for cutting off the pigtail of the young male singer in front of him, what musical figure initially began his career teaching and playing violin in the streets of Vienna?

.... 11

This French composer is generally considered to be the chief representative of impressionism. Who is he? 12

Who produced the most complete recorded Chopin series in history (mid-1930's)?........... 13

Who is known as the "Father of French Piano Music?" 14

The "Andante" of Mozart's *Piano Concerto No. 21* was popularized by what movie in1967?

.... 15

Nicknames have frequently been given to composer's compositions. What are the animal nicknames for these instrumental works?............ 24

   a. String Quartet, *Op. 33, No. 3 in C* by Haydn.

   b. String Quartet, *Op. 50, No. 6 in D* by Haydn.

   c. *Quintet for Piano and Strings in A, D. 667,* by Schubert.

🎵 Why is Haydn's String Quartet, *Op. 55, No. 2 in F Minor* nicknamed "The Razor?" 25

🎵 *Les Vingt-Quatre Violons du Roi* (*The 24 Violins of the King*) was attached to the royal courts of what three French kings?.............................. 26

🎵 Frédéric Chopin's work, *Waltz in D-flat major, Op. 64, No. 1*, bears the common nickname "Minute Waltz." But, this work also has a less-common nickname. Do you know it? 27

🎵 On December 30, 1672, the following adver-tisement was placed in the *London Gazette* by John Banister, a member of *The 24 Violins of the King*: "These are to give notice, that at Mr. John Banister's house (now called the music school) over against the George Tavern, in White Friars, near the back of the Temple, this Monday, will be music performance by excellent masters, beginning precisely at 4 of the clock in the afternoon, and every afternoon in the future, precisely at the same hour." How is this advertisement announcing a musical performance particularly significant?............. 28

🎵 Biblical figure, Miriam, played a hand drum called the timbrel (or tabret) to celebrate an important Biblical event. When did she play this instrument? 29

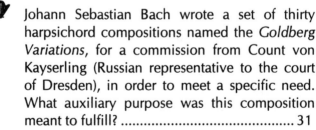

Can you match these pieces that were written for, or are enjoyed by, children with their respective composers? 30
   a) *Tubby the Tuba*
   b) *Carnival of the Animals*
   c) *Children's Corner Suite*
   d) *Babar the Elephant*
   e) *The Little Song that Wanted to be a Symphony*

              Matches with . . .?
   1. Camille Saint-Saëns (1835-1921)
   2. William Grant Still (1895-1978)
   3. George Kleinsinger (born 1914)
   4. Claude Debussy (1862-1918)
   5. Nicolai Berezowsky (1900-1953)

Johann Sebastian Bach wrote a set of thirty harpsichord compositions named the *Goldberg Variations*, for a commission from Count von Kayserling (Russian representative to the court of Dresden), in order to meet a specific need. What auxiliary purpose was this composition meant to fulfill? 31

World-famous violinist, Jascha Heifetz, once boasted to comedic artist, Harpo Marx, that he had earned his living with his violin since the age of five. What was Harpo's famous, anecdotal punchline in response to Heifetz's boasting? 32

Why was Beethoven's second piano concerto written *before* his first piano concerto? 33

What instruments are the following classical artists associated with? 34
   a) William Primrose (born 1904)
   b) Andrés Segovia (born 1893)
   c) E. G. Power Biggs (born 1906)
   d) Larry Adler (born 1914)

He was flute teacher to Frederick the Great, the author of the first comprehensive flute method in the mid-1700's, and the composer of the most flute concertos. Who was he? 35

Name the instruments that bear these distinctions: 36
   a) The most ancient instrument of the human race?
   b) The most popular musical instrument in the home and on the concert stage?
   c) The most glorified and holy musical instrument?
   d) The most ancient wind instrument?

The page turner is a forgotten participant in the world of classical music. However, one American female composer recognized the page turner's importance in a piece entitled, *Trio for Violin, Piano, and Page Turner*. Who was this composer? 37

Pianist Alexander Kelberine made his own suicide a musical, however morbid, event. How did he do this? 38

The popular song, "And This Is My Beloved," from the Broadway musical, *Kismet* (by Robert Wright and George Forrest), received a Tony Award for this 1953 production. This Tony Award, however, rightfully belongs to a classical composer whose *String Quartet No. 2 in D,* was deliberately plagiarized for the song. What composer should rightfully have been awarded this Tony Award, sixty-seven years after his death? 39

Bach studied the works of a Parisian harpsichordist and had great admiration for him. Who was he? 40

Why did Bach, a devoted Lutheran, write the most famous of all Catholic masses, his *Mass in B minor*? 41

One of the movements from Handel's *Fifth Harpsichord Suite* is sometimes referred to as "The Harmonious Blacksmith." The common, but untrue, story is told that Handel named this music after being inspired by the sound of the hammer beating on the anvil when he waited out a storm in a blacksmith's shop. But, Handel had no part in nicknaming this music. How did this music really come to bear this title? 42

🎵 Campanology is the term that denotes what instrumental art form? 43

🎵 A quintet written by one of the greatest composers uses violin, viola, 'cello, double bass, and piano, rather that the typical two violins, viola, and 'cello with piano. Name this quintet and its composer. 44

🎵 In 1721, Bach wrote a set of six concertos on the request of a German prince. This prince, however, unappreciatively left the compositions unopened and in his desk drawer—never to be played until they were found after the prince's death. Paradoxically, the prince's sole claim to fame is his name sake's association with these works. Which Bach works are they?.............. 45

🎵 Who introduced the following novel techniques into keyboard playing: 46
   a) The crossing of hands.
   b) The use of thumbs.
   c) Turning the piano in order to exhibit the musician's profile during performances.

🎵 Norwegian composer, Ole Bull (1810-1880), wrote an unusual composition called "Quartet." How was it unique? 47

Spanish musician, Pablo (Pau) Casals (1876-1973), rose to become one of the premiere cellists, ushering in a new era in the field of cello playing. One of his professional successes was to form one of the world's finest chamber trios in 1905. Along with Casals, who comprised this trio?... 48

In 1923, the first complete string quartet was recorded. Played by the Catterall Quartet, what was the composition?.................................... 49

What is the *Ghost* Trio?................................ 50

How did Schumann devise the title of his *Abegg Variations*? 51

Three pianists . . .

This magnetic concert pianist is said to have been the first performer to exploit his good looks. He would stride onto the stage, flick back his shoulder-length hair, and then remove his gloves and throw them to the floor so that women in the audience would fight to get hold of them. This pianist was, likewise, quite a showman on the keyboard. A key figure in the Romantic era, he exhibited the idea of the artist as hero and is considered to be music's first box-office virtuoso. Who was he? 52

This multi-talented individual was a pianist, composer, and statesman (1860-1941). However, he is most fondly remembered for his compassion and generosity. Much of the wealth that he enjoyed from his professional successes, he gave away to many hundreds of struggling artists. He gave concerts to benefit the Jewish refugees from Nazi Germany, and he gave money to aid his native Poland. Who was he?
.... 53

This Russian pianist (1848-1933) was beloved for his eccentricity. His performances were frequented as much for his execution of Chopin, as for his habit of stopping during a performance to address the audience (or

Answers

1   Admired for his piano music and renowned for his concert theatrics, Franz Liszt (1811-1886) was the creator of the piano recital and the first to give an entire concert using only the piano. The term "recital," however is said to have been first used by F. Beale, Liszt's manager, who felt that Liszt's concerts had a narrative or recitative quality.

2   Henry Purcell (1659-1695) was the first of his profession to be buried at Westminster Abbey and is considered one of the greatest of English composers.

3   Frédéric Chopin (1810-1849).

4   Frederick the Great was a skilled flutist who composed over 100 works for his instrument. He holds the honor of being the composer of the largest number of flute sonatas.

5   Tartini was threatened with arrest for eloping with 15-year-old Elisabetta Premazore.

6   The musical prodigy, Joannes Chrysostomus Wolfgangus Theophilus (or, more commonly known as Wolfgang Amadeus Mozart; 1756-

1791), began composing at the age of three.

7   The term "bagatelle," referring to a short instrumental composition, is generally associated with the composer Beethoven, who wrote several such pieces for the piano, including the popular "Für Elise."

8   Henry V composed church music under the pseudonym, "Roy Henry."

9   Robert Schumann (1810-1856) married the much-younger Clara Wieck (1819-1896) despite her father's initial protest.

10 André Watts (born 1946) first appeared in concert with the Philadelphia Orchestra at the age of nine.

11 Joseph Haydn (1732-1809).

12 Claude Debussy (1862-1918) wrote highly impressionistic works, mostly for solo piano.

13 Artur Rubinstein (1887-1982).

14 François Couperin le Grand (1668-1733).

15 *Elvira Madigan* popularized the second movement of Mozart's *Piano Concerto No. 21.*

16 French composer Erik Satie's (1866-1925) piece, entitled *Vexations*, lasts for less than a minute. But, the composer's notations direct that the piece be played 840 times in non-stop succession. If these instructions were followed, the result would be 14 hours of playing time.

17 John Cage's avant-garde work, *4'33"* (1952), is meant to comprise the unintentional sounds that are produced from inside and outside the concert hall, by the audience and by the people on the street.

18 The most expensive violin ever sold was the 1720 "Mendelssohn" Stradivarius, which was sold by Christie's in London on November 21, 1990 for £902,000 (the equivalent of $1.7 million).

19 A hurdy-gurdy was a popular medieval instrument resembling the lute. Musical sound was produced when a wheel was turned with a handle, causing vibration of the strings. The tune was played on the top string by keys set vertically on the strings. The lower strings supplied the bass.

20 Kirchgessner played on the once-popular glass harmonica, in which tuned glass bowls were suspended in water and rotated by a treadle.

21   Hunting.

22   The Shofar, an ancient type of trumpet fashioned from a ram's horn, is still sounded in the synagogue on the Jewish High Holy Days.

23   Three French horns depict the wolf in this work by Prokofiev.

24   Their nicknames are:
     a. "The Bird"
     b. "The Frog"
     c. "The Trout"

25   Bland, an English publisher, found Haydn having trouble shaving with a dull razor during a visit to Esterhazy. Haydn, swearing to trade his next string quartet for a sharp razor, was quickly given two good razors by Esterhazy. Haydn, in return, dedicated this quartet to him.

26   This was the official "band" of French kings—Louis XIII, Louis XIV, and Louis XV—and was made famous in the 17th century under the direction of conductor Jean-Baptiste Lully.

27   This work by Frédéric Chopin also bears the nickname "The Dog Waltz," because it describes George Sand's dog chasing its tail.

28   This advertisement announced one of the earliest approximations to the modern public concert, particularly what we now call a chamber concert. Rather than relying on a spontaneous tavern audience, Banister formalized this gathering by, first, publicizing the performance and, second, by intentionally seating the musicians on a raised platform and behind drawn curtains. Above all, Banister wished to protect the musicians from being mistaken for mere alehouse serenaders.

29   Miriam, sister to Moses, played the timbrel to celebrate the crossing of the Red Sea.

30   These enjoyable children's pieces were written by these composers: Kleinsinger wrote *Tubby the Tuba*, Saint-Saëns wrote *Carnival of the Animals*, Debussy wrote *Children's Corner Suite*, Berezowsky wrote *Babar the Elephant*, and Still wrote *The Little Song that Wanted to be a Symphony*.

31   Count von Kayserling suffered from insomnia, so he commissioned Bach to compose a work for the clavier that was performed each evening by Bach's pupil, Johann Gottlieb Goldberg, until he was able to fall asleep.

32   Harpo Marx responded "What were you before

that–a bum?" (Besides being a comedic artist, Harpo was also an accomplished harp player–hence the nickname!)

33 Beethoven's "first" piano concerto in C major, was begun in 1795 and finished in 1800. It was published in 1801, as Op. 15. Beethoven's piano concerto in B^b major, Op. 19 was begun before 1793, completed on March 29, 1795, and also published in 1801. Because of its later publication, it became known as the *Second Piano Concerto*.

34 The chosen instruments of these virtuosos are the:
    a) Viola
    b) Guitar
    c) Organ
    d) Harmonica or mouth-organ

35 He was Johann Joachim Quantz (1697-1773), who wrote 300 flute concertos, primarily for his royal student, King Frederick.

36 These instruments are:
    a) Trumpet
    b) Piano
    c) Harp
    d) Flute

37 American composer Pauline Oliveros.

38 Alexander Kelberine included in his last concert program works that only dealt with death. Following the concert, Kelberine returned home and injested a lethal dose of sleeping pills.

39 It was the *Second String Quartet* of Alexander Borodin (1833-1887) that was taken for the award-winning song, "And This Is My Beloved." In fact, almost the entire *Kismet* musical was based on stolen themes from Borodin's works. The "Polovtsian Dances" from Borodin's *Prince Igor* were plagiarized in the two *Kismet* pieces, "Stranger in Paradise" and "He's in Love." Borodin's *Second Symphony* was altered and renamed "Rhymes Have I Fate." And Borodin's *In the Steppes of Central Asia* was transformed into "Sands of Time."

40 Bach highly-esteemed the talents of François Couperin (1668-1733), seventeen years his senior.

41 Bach wrote his *Mass in B Minor* in the hopes of winning the favor of the Elector of Saxony, an important Catholic ruler of the time.

42 A blacksmith living in Bath, England, sang this piece so often that he became known as "the

harmonious blacksmith." A publishing firm then capitalized on the work by printing it under the same title.

43 Campanology is the art of bell ringing.

44 It is Franz Schubert's *Quintet in A major* (or, "*The Trout*").

45 These once-neglected compositions were *The Brandenburg Concertos*, written for the all-but-forgotten Margrave of Brandenburg.

46 These novel keyboard playing techniques were introduced by the following individuals:
   a) Both Domenico Scarlatti and Jean-Philippe Rameau are credited with introducing the crossing of hands into keyboard music.
   b) Bach introduced the use of the thumbs into keyboard performances.
   c) 19th century pianist, Jan Ladislav, had the piano turned so that the audience could see his profile. But, it was Liszt who popularized this practice.

47 Bull wrote *Quartet* for one violin.

48 The trio consisted of Casals, plus Alfred Cortot (pianist) and Jacques Thibaud (violinist).

49   It was Brahm's *String Quartet No. 1 in C minor*, Op. 51, No. 1.

50   This trio is Beethoven's *String Trio No. 4 in D*, Op. 70, No. 1.

51   These variations were dedicated to Countess Abegg, and the themes consisted of the notes A, B flat, E, G, and G.

52   This classical artist was nineteenth century virtuoso pianist Franz Liszt (1811-1886).

53   Ignacy Paderewski.

54   Vladimir de Pachman.

55   *Ein Musikalischer Spass* (*A Musical Joke*) in F major, K. 522; also known as *Dorfmusik* (*The Village Band*).

56   88.

57   The chimes of London's Big Ben Clock Tower.

4

ORCHESTRAL MUSIC

Orchestral music is the most popular form of concert music, judging by the sales of orchestral recordings around the globe. Even so, it is also the musical form that is most resistant to change and innovation. Nicolas Slonimsky, the scholar-chronicler of concert music, writes that "...the musical classics of today were the unmelodious monsters of yesterday" and he estimates that it takes forty years for unfamiliar music to become accepted by the public–"...twenty years to make an artistic curiosity out of a modernistic monstrosity; and another twenty to elevate it to a masterpiece."

In other words, the public dislikes the eccentric and the unusual in the symphonic realm, but learns to accept it anyway. Some of the eccentricities of orchestral composers and works are explored in the forthcoming pages.

Trivia Questions

🎹 Name Igor Stravinsky's work that is used as incidental music for the 'creation of the world' in the Disney film classic, *Fantasia*. 1

🎹 What Afro-American composer was the first to write a classical work of significance which was performed by a major American orchestra?.....2

🎹 What work was described by its composer as "17 minutes of orchestra without any music?"
....3

🎹 This ballet from 1925-1926 was the first attempt to bring Soviet themes onto the stage. Name the ballet and its composer. 4

🎹 Where was America's first permanent symphony orchestra established? What was the name of the orchestra and the individual who founded it?...5

🎹 *Pomp and Circumstance* is the generic title for a set of orchestral marches by Sir Edward Elgar (1857-1934), written for the coronation procession of Edward VII. It is only the middle section of Elgar's first march that is performed at graduation ceremonies all over the United States? To what words did Elgar set this portion of his march?..6

What Italian cellist came to have the greatest single influence on the art of conducting symphony orchestras? 7

The dance number, *The Charleston*, was created by James P. Johnson (1891-1955), and it first appeared in the Harlem Broadway revue "Runnin' Wild" in 1923. What composer orchestrated this popular dance in the early part of his career?...8

This Russian composer incorporated new technology into his last orchestral work based on the Greek myth of Prometheus. Name this composer and the innovative technology he utilized? 9

Who was the first composer to incorporate the *Blues* idiom in a major symphonic work? 10

The London Symphony Orchestra was founded in 1904, and, a few years later, began an era of intercontinental tours. In 1912, these tours were almost cut short before their time. What tragedy did the entire membership of the 1912 London Symphony Orchestra narrowly avoid?........... 11

What are the animal nicknames often used to

refer to Haydn's *Symphony No. 82 in C major* and *Symphony No. 83 in G minor*, respectively?.. 12

The movie *10* starring Bo Derek popularized this classic work. Name the work and the composer?.. 13

Where did the gamelan orchestra originate?
.... 14

The performance of what composition resulted in the most famous riot in musical history?.... 15

During the German siege of Leningrad in World War I (summer of 1941), Dmitri Shostakovitch composed his seventh symphony, appropriately nicknamed *The Leningrad Symphony*. While composing this symphony, Shostakovitch also had an important military duty to perform. What was this duty? 16

Due to technological restrictions, recordings of music prior to 1925 were of a shorter duration. However, a development in the mid-1920's allowed for recordings that were longer in length. What was this development?............. 17
In the late 1940's, an invention allowed longer musical works, such as symphonies, to be

Sporting events and pasttimes have made an appearance in several orchestral works. Do you know the sporting events or pasttimes that have been featured in these compositions?............ 19

    a. *Half-Time* by Bohuslav (Jan) Martinů.

    b. *Jeux* by Debussy.

    c. *Jeu de Cartes* by Stravinsky.

    d. *Susannens Geheimnis* by Wolf-Ferrari.

    e. *La Traviata* by Verdi.

How many strings does the harp have? And why was the harp prevented from joining the orchestra prior to the 19th century?............... 20

Erik Satie (1866-1925) was one of the first composers to incorporate non-musical sounds in his compositions. His ballet music, *Parade*, includes what non-traditional sounds? 21

John Alden Carpenter's symphonic suite, *Seven Ages* (1945), was inspired by what Shakespearean play? 22

The visual arts have also been known to inspire composers to write certain pieces. What two separate artistic works inspired George Antheil's *Symphony No. 6* (world premiere given 1949) and John Alden Carpenter's ballet piece, entitled *Krazy Kat* (1921)? 23

On what orchestral instruments do you find "nuts," "scrolls," and "ribs?" 24

Name at least one composer of great operas who wrote only one symphony. 25

Berlin was the musical center of Europe in the 1920's. The Berlin Philharmonic Orchestra, however, performed in a concert hall that had originally served another function in the mid-nineteenth century. What was its original function? 26

What orchestral works suggest the following, non-traditional sounds? 27
   a) The ticking of a metronome?
   b) The ticking of a clock?
   c) The beating of raindrops on a roof?
   d) Knocking at a door?

The classical symphony has four movements, but there have been exceptions to this rule. Name a symphony with . . .
   a) One movement?
   b) Two movements?
   c) Three movements?
   d) Five movements?
   e) Ten movements?

Orchestral Music

a) *The First of a Few*
b) *2001: A Space Odyssey*
c) *Death in Venice*
d) *The Horse's Mouth*

Matches with . . .

1) Mahler's *Fourth Symphony in G major*
2) Prokofiev's *Lieutenant Kijé*
3) Strauss' *Thus Spake Zarathustra*
4) Sir William Walton's *Spitfire* Prelude and Fugue

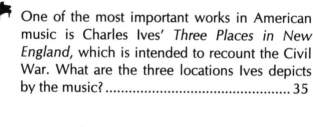

One of the most important works in American music is Charles Ives' *Three Places in New England*, which is intended to recount the Civil War. What are the three locations Ives depicts by the music? 35

Who is the only composer to have written a symphony in the key of D-flat major?............ 36

Beethoven's *Symphony No. 3*, the "Eroica," bears an Italian inscription that pays homage to what historical figure? 37

A princely patron who wished to stay in Esterhazy would not allow the players of his royal orchestra to go home to Vienna. With a longing to return home, and with humorous intent, the court composer wrote a unique symphony. The work began gaily, but came to a sorrowful conclusion. In the end, the musicians left the platform one by one, each blowing out a candle by his music stand before exiting, until one player, the composer himself, was left to finish the plaintive music amidst a single flicking candlelight. The prince understood the composer's intention and was persuaded to let the players of the royal orchestra return to Vienna. What symphony is this and by whom?
.... 38

In 1950 wartime-Korea, Chinese communists used the music of Wagner's opera *Lohengrin* as an instrument of war against British and American soldiers. How did they do this?............... 39

When first performed in Paris (1926), and then in New York (1927), George Antheil's *Ballet mécanique* shocked the public with its novel use of sound. What are some of the unusual sounds that Antheil incorporated into this work? 40

What orchestral instrument provides the pitch "A 440" for tuning before a concert?............. 41

Can you name a piano concerto which has four movements, instead of the traditional three? . 42

The open, creative facility of many orchestral composers has inspired them to include unusual instruments in some of their orchestral works. What unconventional music-maker is asked for in each of these compositions?....... 43
  a) Strauss' *Don Quixote* & *Alpine Symphony*
  b) Gershwin's *An American in Paris*
  c) Tchaikovsky's *1812 Overture*
  d) Respighi's *The Pines of Rome*
  e) Still's *Afro-American Symphony*

She is credited with being the first American female to write a symphony. Who is she? 44

The following composers were the first of their

ethnic distinction to write a major symphonic work. Can you name the symphony and/or approximately when it was composed?......... 45
- Joãn Domingos Bomtempo (Portuguese)
- Axel Gabriel Ingelius (Finnish)
- Ricardo Castro (Mexican)

 Match these composers with their corresponding distinctions:.. 46
- a) Wrote the first cello concerto
- b) Wrote the first violin concerto
- c) Wrote the first piano concerto
- d) Wrote the most violin concertos
- e) Wrote the most flute concertos

Matches . . .
1. Antonio Vivaldi
2. Giuseppe Torelli
3. Johann Joachim Quartz
4. Johann Sebastian Bach
5. Jacchini

 On the afternoon of "Pearl Harbor Day" (December 7, 1941), thousands were listening to the New York Philharmonic broadcast over the radio. At the time that the broadcast was interrupted with the catastrophic news of the attack, what piano concerto was Artur Rubinstein performing? 47

When Warner Brothers produced a movie in which a female was seduced while a composition by Igor Stravinsky was played, the composer protested by suing the movie production company. A court judge in Paris, France, however, did not feel that the music had been defamed, and awarded Stravinsky a token sum of one franc. Which of Stravinsky's works was used in the movie?...................... 48

In what ballet do you find Cinderella and her Prince, Puss-in-Boots, Little Red Riding Hood, and Hop-o-my-Thumb? 49

Hungarian composer, Zoltán Kodály (1882-1967) composed an opera entitled, *Háry János*, based on the tale of the great liar of Hungarian folklore and his love for Napolean's second wife. Kodály later arranged the material into an orchestral suite. In what humorous way does this suite begin?... 50

Well-known British composer, Ralph Vaughan Williams (1872-1958) wrote, *Symphony No. 2*, or *A London Symphony*, in the early 1900's. What famous London attraction is simulated in this symphony? 51

As played by Arthur Nikisch and the Berlin Philharmonic Orchestra, what was the first complete symphony recorded? 52

Answers

1   Igor Stravinsky's *Le Sacre du printemps* (*The Rite of Spring*) accompanied the ancient geologic events depicted in this Disney classic. [Interestingly, Stravinsky's composition doesn't cover up Disney's paleontological error in this segment of the film. A portion of the film segment shows a Tyrannosaurus Rex of the Cretaceous period fighting a Stegosaurus of the Jurassic period. Such a battle could never have taken place since these species lived in paleontological periods approximately ninety million years apart.]

2   William Grant Still (1895-1978) earned this important honor when his *Afro-American Symphony* was performed at an American Composers' Concert at the Eastman School of Music under the baton of Dr. Howard Hanson on October 29, 1931.

3   Maurice Ravel (1875-1937) described his composition *Boléro*, based on a Spanish dance, in this way.

4   The ballet supported by Soviet ideology is *The Age of Steel* (1925-1926), and was composed by Serge Prokofiev (1891-1953).

5   The first permanent symphony orchestra in the United States was established in New York (1842) by Ureli Corelli Hill, and was known as the Philharmonic Society of New York. Later the orchestra was combined with the New York Symphony Society and is today known as the New York Philharmonic-Symphony Orchestra.

6   The middle section of Elgar's first march from the *Pomp and Circumstance* trio is set to the words "Land of Hope and Glory." (The title *Pomp and Circumstance* comes from Shakespeare's *Othello*).

7   Cellist Arturo Toscanini's (1867-1957) influence on the art of conducting started quite by accident when he filled in as conductor at the last minute for an 1886 event.

8   American composer, William Grant Still (1895-1978), orchestrated this popular dance while he was living and working in New York.

9   Alexander Scriabin (1872-1915) used colored lights combined with the music in his last orchestral work, entitled *Prometheus: the Poem of Fire*, in 1819.

10 William Grant Still (1895-1978) was the first to

use Blues-inspired themes and harmonies in a symphonic composition.

11 The members of the 1912 London Symphony Orchestra had booked passage on the maiden voyage of the *S.S. Titantic*. However, the symphony's agent rescheduled their New York tour to start two days earlier, which required that the orchestra members sail on the *S.S. Baltic*. Thus, they avoided the tragic sinking of the *S.S. Titantic* on April 15, 1912.

12 "L'Ours" ("The Bear") and "La Poule" ("The Hen").

13 Maurice Ravel's *Bolero* enjoyed a resurgence of popularity with this movie.

14 The gamelan orchestra is the orchestra of Indonesia.

15 The world premiere of Stravinsky's ballet, *La Sacre du printemps* (*The Rite of Spring*), at the Théâtre des Champs-Elyssées in 1913, resulted in a full-blown riot. The music was thought to be barbaric, and the dancing to be of an unacceptably erotic nature.

16 Shostakovitch (1906-1975) was enlisted as a fire-watcher during this military crisis.

17 The development of electrical recording devices made it possible to record orchestral works.

18 The invention of the long-playing disc in the late 1940's enabled longer works to be recorded on a single record, instead of being spread over several records.

19 The sporting events or pasttimes are:
    a. Soccer
    b. Tennis
    c. Poker
    d. Smoking
    e. Drinking

20 The harp's lack of musical range prevented it from joining the orchestra. However, during the 19th century, Sebastian Érard perfected the pedal mechanism of the harp and, thus, increased the range of its 47 strings.

21 Satie's *Parade* incorporates the sound of a ship's foghorn and the clattering of typewriters.

22 Shakespeare's *As You Like It* inspired Carpenter to compose this symphonic piece.

23 Antheil's *Symphony No. 6* was inspired by Eugene Delacroix's painting "Liberty Leading the People," and Carpenter's *Krazy Kat* is one of

the few symphonic pieces to be inspired by a comic strip–George Herriman's "Krazy Kat" comic strip.

24 Violins, violas, celli, and double basses.

25 Opera composer Richard Wagner wrote an early symphony, and Bizet composed the *Symphony in C.*

26 The Philharmonic concert hall had originally served as a rollerskating rink.

27 These sounds are suggested in:
   a) Beethoven's *Symphony No. 8.*
   b) Haydn's *Symphony No. 101 in D major.*
   c) Chopin's *Prelude, Op. 28,* "Raindrop."
   d) Beethoven's *Symphony No. 5.*

28 Symphonies that have been composed in disregard for the standard, four-movement guideline are:
   a) Sibelius' *Symphony No. 7.*
   b) Schubert's *Symphony No. 8* or *Unfinished Symphony.*
   c) César Auguste Franck's *Symphony in D minor,* and many early symphonies by Mozart, Haydn, and others.
   d) Berlioz's *Symphonie Fantastique.*

e) Messiaen's *Turangalîla Symphony*.

f) Norman Rutherlyn's *A Legend in Music of the Life and Times of Sir Winston Churchill* has the most movements ever written into a symphony. If the symphony were ever performed, it would take 2½ hours to play.

29 An August Wilhelmj arrangement of the second movement of this Bach composition was given the nickname *Air on the G String*, in which the first violin part became a solo with accompaniment, and was transposed so as to be suitable for playing on the lowest (and thickest) string of the instrument. American nightclub customers are thought to have given the arrangement its vulgar association.

30 Derived from the ancient Greek tongue, "orchestra" means "place for dancing." Just as the dancers and instrumentalists in the ancient Greek theatres formed a semi-circle between the audience and the stage, the present day orchestra is seated in a half-circle in the modern concert hall.

31 Composer Johann Stamitz was the first to include the clarinet in an orchestral score.

32 The toys used as musical instruments in this

symphony were a rattle, a triangle, and several squeaker toys.

33 Barber's popular *Adagio for Strings* was played at Franklin Delano Roosevelt's funeral in April 1945, and it was used in the movie about the Vietnam War, entitled *Platoon*.

34 Sir Walton's "Spitfire" was used in *The First of a Few*; Strauss' *Thus Spake Zarathustra* was used in *2001: A Space Odyssey*; Mahler's *Fourth Symphony in G major* was used in *Death in Venice*; and Prokofiev's *Lieutenant Kijé* was used in *The Horse's Mouth*.

35 This piece by Charles Ives depicts the St. Gauden's monument in Boston Common, Putnam's Camp in Redding, Connecticut, and the Housatonic at Stockbridge.

36 Nikolai Yakovlevich Miaskovsky's (1881-1950) *Symphony No. 25* (1946) is written in this key.

37 Beethoven, who denounced Napolean after he declared himself Emperor in May 1804, initially dedicated this symphony to him.

38 Haydn's *Symphony No. 45*, or the "Farewell Symphony," written in 1772, was used to play this prank on Prince Esterhazy.

39 The Chinese played the music of Wagner's opera, *Lohengrin*, for British and American soldiers in order to scare them away from the northwest Korean front. As an American soldier recounted in a news bulletin, "I was one of 500 men who fought their way out of a Chinese Communist trap. ...Around 9 p.m., an eerie sound sent shivers along my spine. A lone bugler on a ridge one hundred yards away was playing Lohengrin's [music]. A Chinese voice speaking English floated across the valley, saying: "That's for you, boys–you won't ever hear it again."

40 George Antheil's *Ballet mécanique* incorporates the novel sounds of anvils, airplane propellers, motor horns, buzz saws, and electric bells.

41 The oboe.

42 Brahms' *Concerto No. 2 in B-flat major*.

43 These composers asked for: a) wind and thunder machines, b) an automobile horn, c) a cannon, d) a phonograph record, and e) a banjo.

44 Amy Marcy Beach (or, commonly known as Mrs. H. H. Beach; 1867-1944) was the first American female to write a symphony. Her *Gaelic Symphony* was composed in 1894.

45 Bomtempo wrote the *E flat Symphony* (c. 1800), Ingelius wrote the first Finnish symphony in 1847, and Castro wrote his *Symphony No. 1* in 1883.

46 Jacchini wrote the first cello concerto, Torelli wrote the first violin concerto, Bach wrote the first piano concerto, Vivaldi wrote the most violin concerti, and Quartz wrote the most flute concerti.

47 Your memory serves you well if you got this one—Rubinstein conducted Brahms' *Concerto No. 2 in B-flat*.

48 It was Stravinsky's *Firebird*.

49 The names of these fairy tale characters are the titles for the movements of Tchaikovsky's *The Sleeping Beauty*.

50 This suite begins with a simulated "sneeze" by the orchestra.

51 The chimes of London's Big Ben Clock Tower.

52 Beethoven's *Symphony No. 5 in C minor*.

5

COMPOSERS AND CONDUCTORS

$\mathfrak{C}$lassical music is realized from the most modest of resources. Composers have only a pallet of their own creativity, a writing implement, and paper to call their "instruments." Conductors rely on their own authoritative stature and the other musical artists who constitute the orchestras they lead. From these simple provisions, come enumerable pleasures for the classical music patron.

Writer and critic, H. L. Mencken, noted that, "Music is kind to its disciples. When they bring high talents to its service, they are not forgotten." So, let's explore the "firsts," the eccentricities, and the real-life drama of some of those individuals who seek to raise music to its highest form.

Trivia Questions

♫ Name three composers who wrote symphonic scores inspired by Shakespeare's *Romeo and Juliet*? 1

♫ Composer Josef Mysliveček (1737-1781), known as "il divino Boemo" ("the divine Bohemian"), was the victim of a misguided doctor who prescribed a quack cure for his venereal disease. What upper body part was surgically removed from Mysliveček, to make him the only composer without one of these? 2

♫ What English royal personage, historically known for his domestic "disputes," composed two masses (now lost) and several short pieces, including an arrangement of a song for three voices entitled *Pastyme with good companye*?

....3

♫ Composer Johann Sebastian Bach fathered how many children, and how many survived to adulthood? And, of those who survived, how many pursued the music profession? 4

♫ This Afro-American conductor was the first to conduct a major symphony orchestra in the

116

XIV and made Versailles an important center for opera and ballet, died of a self-inflicted, but accidental, injury in 1687? What was this injury? 11

Who is regarded as the "Father of Russian Music?" 12

Who was the first Afro-American to conduct a major radio orchestra in the United States? ... 13

Who is heralded as the "English Mozart?" 14

In 1877, Nadezhda von Meck, a widow with 11 children, offered to provide composer Peter Ilyich Tchaikovsky with generous annual subsidies, but on one condition? What was this condition and why was it mandatory? 15

The lightweight baton used by modern-day conductors was introduced at a London rehearsal in 1820 by whom? 16

With over 800 recordings of all major works to his credit, he is said to be the most recorded conductor ever. Name this conductor. 17

The most Grammy Awards, totaling 31 in all,

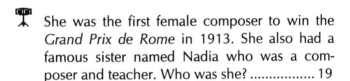

✠ Scenes from this composer's operas were put in huge pictorials on the walls of Ludwig II's Bavarian castle. Can you name this composer and the castle that was used to illustrate his musical creations? 20

✠ The brilliant 19th century French pianist-composer, Charles Henri Valentin Alkan's real name was Morhange. In spite of his musical brilliance, he avoided life in the public eye. He died in unusual circumstances. How did Alkan die? 21

✠ What was the common item used to conduct prior to the adoption of the baton? 22

✠ The Strauss family is associated with the waltz. Can you name all four members of this Austrian family who are recognized composers? 23

✠ In hiring an employee who was not his first choice for the job, a Leipzig employer once said, "Since the best man could not be obtained, mediocre ones would have to be accepted." Who was the object of this unflattering assessment? 24

✠ The composers Emmanuel Chabier, Gaetano

Beethoven began to lose this faculty at the age of 28. Some years later, he lost it completely. What was this faculty?...................................... 31

Who was America's first Afro-American woman composer of international stature?................. 32

What musical figures comprised the 19th century Russian nationalist composers' group known as "The Five" (or, in Russia, known as the *moguchaya kuchka* or the *mighty handful*)?
.... 33
Can you also name the part-time professions these individuals pursued during their lives?
.... 34

Conductor Hans von Bülow is credited with coining the phrase, "The Three B's." To whom was Bülow referring?.................................... 35

When the conductor Sir Thomas Beecham was facing a problematic performance of *Aïda*, including a camel that relieved itself on the stage during the triumphal scene, he made a humorous, well-remembered comment. What was this remark?.. 36

Tchaikovsky had difficulty reconciling himself

to an aspect of his life that was perhaps complicated by a brief and disastrous marriage as well as the ardent admiration and financial support of a wealthy widow. What was Tchaikovsky's personal dilemma? 37

Besides pursuing musical interests, what professional status did American composer Charles Ives (1874-1954) hold? 38

When the first performance was held at the Metropolitan Opera in 1883, he was the conductor. Who was the individual who conducted the Met's first performance?............... 39

In the 1600's, she was the first female composer to write an opera. Do you know her name and the name of the opera that she composed? ... 40

Somewhat of a child prodigy, this English composer and musical historian was said at the age of five to be able to recognize the key in which his father blew his nose. At age six, he played a duet with Mendelssohn. Who was he?

.... 41

Under what political circumstances did Spanish composer Enrique Granados (1867-1916) die?

.... 42

Following the lead of Vladimir Stasov's group, "The Five," and to complement the nationalist trend of the day, critic Henri Collet coined the phrase, "Les Six" (or "The Six"), after this group of composers published an album of musical works together. Name the six French composers who comprised this group. 43

During his appointment as organist at Arnstadt's Bonifacius-Kirche, Johann Sebastian Bach was severely reprimanded by his employer in 1706, after he was granted temporary leave. Why?

Great composers have been known to make prophetic or predictive statements about the talents of up-and-coming composers. Identify the subjects of the following words of praise:

Mozart once said of him, "Keep your eyes on him; some day he will give the world something to talk about." Who was the subject of this comment?

Of this composer, Schumann once said, "Hats off, gentlemen–a genius!" Toward what person was this comment directed?

Haydn was heard to remark about this person, "I declare to you before God, as a man of honor, that your son is the greatest composer I know, either personally, or by reputation." Of whom was Haydn speaking?

Rudolf Karel (1880-1945), a devoted Czech-oslovakian composer and the last student of Antonin Dvorák, composed until his tragic death. Where did Karel sketch his final work, *Three Hairs of a Wise Old Man*?

🎼 Who was the first composer of rank to depend on the sale of sheet music and concert performances for much of his income?.................. 49

🎼 What German composer, with whom the Romantic movement in opera was launched, had to flee France in order to escape debtor's prison? 50

🎼 This Italian composer of opera was born in Leap Year on February 29th, and, hence, only had a calendar birthday every four years. This same composer was highly superstitious and feared Fridays that fell on the 13th day of the month. Ironically, he died in Paris on Friday, November 13, 1868. Who was he?............... 51

🎼 Like the composer in question #51, this composer suffered from triskaidekaphobia, the fear of the number 13. He was disturbed by the fact that he was born on the 13th of the month and consciously omitted the number 13 from the numbered bars of his compositions. For his opera, *Moses und Aaron*, he deleted the second *a* in *Aaron* (making it *Aron*) when he realized that the number of letters in the title totalled 13. Further, he was shaken when an insensitive person reminded him on his 76th birthday that

7 plus 6 equalled 13. He died on July 13, 1951, 13 minutes before midnight, at the age of 76. Who was he? 52

The genius of song, Franz Schubert (1797-1828), expressed a desire to read the novels of what author during his last and fatal illness in Vienna, 1828? 53

Who is revered as the "Dean of Afro-American Composers?" 54

In the early 19th century, a talented young woman pursued her interest in composing. Felix Mendelssohn included some of her art songs in a collection of his own works, because he did not feel that it was appropriate for a woman to be published or to have a musical career outside the home. He was taken aback when Queen Victoria unknowingly chose "Italien" as her favorite song, forcing Mendelssohn to admit that they were not his art songs. Who was this female composer? 55

This celebrated composer once boasted, "Give me a laundry list and I will set it to music." But, although he wrote many prominent operas during the first half of his life, he did not write a single work for the stage in the second half of his life. Name this composer of opera?.......... 56

Who is acknowledged as the first native-born, American composer-musician of color to achieve world-wide recognition? 57

How did the expression "face the music" come about? 58

William Billings (1746-1800) is recognized as the first native-born, American composer of significance. Diarist William Bentley acclaimed Billings as "the father of our new England music." A tanner by trade, Billings was unable to fight in the Revolutionary War because of his physical disabilities. Instead, he wrote march music for the war effort. Interestingly, it has also been said that Billings was America's first traffic controller. How did Billings serve in this capacity? 59

Commonly, the music of many great innovators is unappreciated by the public in the composers' lifetimes and is often criticized as being "noise." Such a criticism is made when one of the characters in Oscar Wilde's novel, *The Picture of Dorian Gray*, says, "I like _____'s (a composer's name) music better than anybody's. It is so loud that one can talk the whole time without other people hearing what one says." Who was Wilde's character speaking of? 60

The works of certain composers have been cataloged by others using a letter-number notation. The letter refers to the last name of the cataloger. Name the individuals who cataloged the works of these composers? 61
   a) "K:" The cataloging of Mozart's works *or* the second cataloging of Domenico Scarlatti's compositions.
   b) "L:" The first cataloging of Scarlatti's works.
   c) "S:" The catalog of Bach's works.
   d) "D:" The catalog of Schubert's works.

Who are the famous composers who have been referred to as the following?: 62
   a) "The Prince of Music" or "The Homer of Music"
   b) "Lump" (a nickname)
   c) "The Music Christ"
   d) "Titan, the Prometheus of Music"

Who was the composer best known to his contemporaries of the 1700's? (Hint: It was not Bach.).. 63

What aspiring, young composer, who later achieved notoriety, lived with composer Robert Schumann and carried on an affectionate, but "undefined," relationship with his wife, pianist Clara Schumann? 64

What composer incorporated a bit of the patriotic song, "Yankee Doodle," in one of his most famous compositions?.......................... 65

One of the greatest conductors of all time, he served as conductor of the Rio de Janeiro Opera, as chief conductor for both the La Scala Opera House in Milan and the Metropolitan Opera House in New York, and as the first conductor of radio's NBC Symphony Orchestra. Who was he? 66

Female composer, Amy Marcy Beach, is credited with being the first American woman to achieve notoriety as a composer of serious music, and was given an important distinction by *Étude* magazine. What was this honorary distinction?.. 67

When Cathrine Felicie van Rees, a 19th century-composer generally known for her operettas, wrote *Kent gij dat volk vol heldenmold* (or, *Know Ye This Race of Bravery*) in 1875, she became the first and only female composer to ever write one of these. What type of composition did Rees write? 68

What romantically-bold 17th century Italian composer-violinist-singer, noted for being one of the world's first symphonists, died at the hands of hired assassins, following his elopement with the mistress of an important Venetian nobleman? 69

Felipe Pedrell (1841-1922) kindled a nationalist movement during his life, and encouraged developing composers to draw upon the folk music of their land to inspire their musical works. In his day, where would you have found Pedrell? 70

What Afro-American became the first to conduct a major symphony orchestra in the deep South, when he led the New Orleans Philharmonic at Southern University in 1955? 71

Can you match these composers with an unusual circumstance in their lives?: 72
  a) George Antheil
  b) Benjamin Carr
  c) Don Carlo Gesualdo
  d) Howard Hanson
          Matches with . . .
  1) He ordered the murder of his unfaithful wife and her lover.
  2) At 19, he was a college professor. At 22, he was Dean of Fine Arts. He was the first to win the American Prix de Rome.

3) Besides being a composer, he was an endo-crinologist, a love-advice columnist for a Chicago newspaper, and the author of a book on international war strategy.

4) He opened the first music store in America.

🎼 This composer, known for his innovative use of the synthesizer in the popular recording "Switched-On-Bach," was the first composer known to have undergone a sex-change opera-tion. Who is he (now she)?........................... 73

🎼 This 19th-century Russian pianist and composer was well-received when he arrived on tour in America in 1872. However, some remember him for his pecularity in being such a sound sleeper that normal coaxing would not wake him. The only way that his wife could wake him was to play an unresolved chord on the piano. Unable to stand it, he would rush to the piano to resolve the chord. While doing this, his wife would remove all the coverings from the bed so that he could not get back in. Who was the composer with this unusual sleeping habit? 74

🎼 *A genius nearly lost . . .*
Born in a village outside of Parma, Italy, in 1814, this great composer's mother fled to a

nearby church with him as a infant, with other women and children from the area. The frightened women and children sought a safe place while invading forces ransacked their village. Their refuge was short-lived as soldiers forced open the church doors and killed all the woman and children in sight. One woman with her infant son, however, managed to escape to the belfry, where she hid until the danger had passed. Who was the composer thus saved from death? 75

Born in Stockholm (1694-1758), he wrote twenty-one symphonies, twenty violin sonatas, a few concertos, and a number of other works. He is known as the "Father of Swedish Music." Who was he? 76

On the dark side . . .
This composer was born in a derelict house on the "Street of the Black Cat." When he was five, his exhilaration when he borrowed his brother's violin caused him to faint and go into a trance for two days. So skilled was he at the violin in his professional years that one French critic said, "Had he played like that a century ago, he would have been burned as a sorcerer." And, in fact, he was imprisoned for eight years, and his violin was taken away, because he was thought

to be in league with the Devil and, hence, a danger to others. Name this violinist-composer?

Answers

1   Berlioz, Prokofiev, and Tchaikovsky were inspired by Shakespeare's play, *Romeo and Juliet*.

2   Mysliveček is the only known composer who didn't have a nose.

3   King Henry VIII is known to have been a composer, however of no great distinction, and he wrote a number of short musical compositions.

4   Bach was father to 20 children, 10 of which survived to adulthood. Of those who survived, four sons took up music as a profession.

5   William Grant Still (1895-1978) earned the respect of the White-dominated world of music and became the first Afro-American to conduct a major symphony orchestra in the United States.

6   Thomas Tallis (1505?-1585) was among the first to write for the English church.

7   Antonio Vivaldi proved to be a prolific composer in the 18th century at the *Pio Ospedale della Pieta* orphanage in Venice. An unverified

story tells how Vivaldi, in his later years, was summoned before the Inquisition because he was said to have interrupted a mass by rushing into his office to write down a musical idea before he forgot it. The Inquisition deemed him unfit to celebrate mass from then on.

8   This significant festival took place in the Spring of 1978.

9   Bedřich Smetana (1824-1884).

10   Wolfgang Amadeus Mozart (1756-1791).

11   While conducting in Paris, Lully accidentally struck his foot with the long, heavy staff that he was beating on the floor to keep the tempo. An abscess developed, which became complicated by gangrene, and caused the 54-year-old to die of blood poisoning.

12   Mikhail Glinka (1804-1857) composed the first national Russian opera, *A Life for the Tsar*, or under the title it bears today, *Ivan Susanin*.

13   William Grant Still (1895-1978) was the first of his race to conduct a major radio orchestra, in the early 1930's, when he conducted for Willard Robison's "Deep River Hour" broadcast

on WOR in New York.

14 William Crotch (1775-1847), like Mozart, was a musical prodigy who, at the age of 2 years and 3 months, could play the national anthem on a homemade organ, and, who was giving daily organ recitals in London by the age of four (1779).

15 The condition required by Madame von Meck was that Tchaikovsky and she never meet. Madame von Meck did not want to risk meeting her idol and being disillusioned by the encounter.

16 German composer-conductor Ludwig (Louis) Spohr (1784-1859) is credited with the introduction of today's conductor's instrument. When Mendelssohn later introduced Liepzig to the baton in 1835, the idea was still a novelty.

17 The principal conductor of the Berlin Philharmonic Orchestra for 35 years was prolific Austrian conductor, Herbert von Karajan (1908-1989).

18 Sir Georg Solti (born 1912), principal conductor of the Chicago Symphony Orchestra, has set the record for Grammy Awards received.

19 Composer Lili Juliette Marie Olga Boulanger (1893-1918) won the prize with her cantata, *Fanor et Hélène*.

20 The music of Richard Wagner was the object of King Ludwig II's admiration, and it was on the walls of Neuschwanstein that his artist painted scenes from Wagner's operatic works.

21 The pianist-composer Charles Alkan (1813-1888) was a devoted Jewish scholar. He died when a bookcase crushed him when he tried to remove a volume of the *Talmud* from the top shelf.

22 A rolled-up piece of paper or sheet music was used prior to the introduction of the baton in the 19th century.

23 The Strauss family is associated with Viennese dance music, or the waltz. Johann, his son Johann Jr., and his brothers, Josef and Eduard, all have been recognized as composers of varying degrees of competence.

24 As was the case with many composers in their day, the musical genius of Johann Sebastian Bach (1685-1750) was not appreciated by others during his lifetime.

25 The deaths of all of these composers were hastened by mental instability.

26 "At the pianoforte" was the expression commonly used prior to the adoption of the term "conductor."

27 Franz Joseph Haydn (1732-1809).

28 Leonard Bernstein (1918-1990) was the first American to conduct at Milan's La Scala.

29 Filtz had a taste for spiders.

30 Composers Kodály, Bartók, and Ligeti are considered to be the three major figures in Hungarian music in this century.

31 By 1819, Beethoven had completely lost his hearing.

32 Florence Price (1888-1953).

33 This nationalist group was comprised of Balakirev, Borodin, Cui, Mussorgsky, and Rimsky-Korsakov. This group was formed by Zaremba, a teacher of composition at a conservatory in St. Petersburg, who was dedicated to developing a uniquely Russian style quite

unlike the prevailing European style of composition.

34 Balakirev was a railway official; Borodin, a chemist and scientist; Cui, a military engineer; Mussorgsky, an army officer then a civil servant; and Rimsky-Korsakov, a naval officer.

35 Bülow's "Three B's" are Bach, Beethoven, and Brahms.

36 Beecham was heard to exclaim, "Terribly vulgar, but, Lord, what a critic!"

37 Tchaikovsky had difficulty reconciling his homosexual orientation. However, he eventually addressed his personal dilemma by becoming one of the first major composers to make his sexual orientation known to the public.

38 Charles Ives was a New York insurance company executive. He began selling insurance after leaving Yale in 1898.

39 The Italian conductor, Cleofonte Campanini (1860-1919).

40 She was Francesca Caccini (1587-1640), and her opera bore the lengthy title of *La*

Liberazione di Ruggiero dall'Isola d'Alcina (or, *The Liberation of Ruggiero from the Island of Alcina*).

41 This English individual was Frederick Arthur Gore Ousely (1825-1889).

42 Granados was returning from the world premiere of his opera, *Goyescas*, which had been held at the New York Metropolitan Opera, when a German submarine sank his ship, the S.S. Sussex, in the English Channel.

43 "The Six" was comprised of Georges Auric (1899-1983), Louis Durey (1888-1979), Arthur Honegger (1892-1955), Darius Milhaud (1892-1974), Francis Poulenc (1899-1963), and Germaine Tailleferre (1892-1983).

44 Bach was granted a month's leave to see Buxtehude in Lübeck, the most famous composer of that time, in North Germany. However, Bach, for lack of money, had to make the 200-mile-long journey on foot. He did not return to Arnstadt until sixteen weeks later– three months behind schedule.

45 Mozart made his comment in reference to Ludwig van Beethoven, after the sixteen-year-old Beethoven had improvised for him in Vienna.

46 Schumann expressed his admiration for Chopin with this statement.

47 Haydn said these words in reference to Mozart.

48 Karel sketched this final work at Terezin, a Nazi concentration camp. It was arranged and performed posthumously in 1948 in Prague.

49 Ludwig von Beethoven (1770-1827).

50 Carl Maria von Weber (1786-1826).

51 Gioacchino Antonio Rossini (1792-1868).

52 Arnold Schoenberg (1874-1951).

53 Schubert wished to read the works of James Fenimore Cooper.

54 William Grant Still (1895-1978) is distinguished as the "Dean of Afro-American Composers."

55 The composer was the older sister of Felix, Fanny Cecilia Mendelssohn Hensel, wife of a noted court painter, Wilhelm Hensel, and a pianist.

56 Gioacchino Antonio Rossini (1792-1868) was a source of perplexity when, after composing almost forty operas in fifteen years, he only

produced a few minor compositions in the second half of his life. When asked why he stopped composing operas, Rossini walked casually over to his pianoforte, played a well-loved passage from *Don Giovanni*, and said, "There, my dear friend, to compose music after such as that is simply to carry water to a springing well."

57 Composer and virtuoso pianist, Louis Moreau Gottschalk (1829-1869).

58 In the early days of conducting, it was the practice to face the audience rather than the members of the orchestra. Later, realizing that there was a need to exercise control over the musicians, conductors abandoned the social code of politeness not to turn one's back to the public, and "faced the music."

59 As traffic controller, William Billings was commissioned to keep hogs off the streets.

60 Wagner was the object of this unflattering remark.

61 The individuals who conscientiously cataloged these composers' works were:
  a) Austrian musical bibliographer, Ludwig von Köchel (1800-1877) cataloged the

works of Mozart. American harpsichordist and musicologist, Ralph Kirkpatrick (born 1911) cataloged Scarlatti's works.

b) Italian pianist, Alessandro Longo (1864-1945) first attempted the cataloging of Scarlatti's works.

c) Bach's works were cataloged by German musicologist, Wolfgang Schmieder (1900-1973).

d) The works of Schubert were cataloged by German musicologist, Otto Deutsch.

62 They are:
   a) Giovanni da Palestrina (1525-1594)
   b) Wolfgang Mozart (1756-1791)
   c) Wolfgang Mozart (1756-1791)
   d) Ludwig van Beethoven (1770-1827)

63 Known as the "Father of Sacred Music" in his day, Georg Telemann (1681-1767) enjoyed great popularity as a composer while alive. Ironically, Bach, who was largely unappreciated during his lifetime, now overshadows the all-but-forgotten Telemann.

64 Johannes Brahms.

65 Antonin Dvořák.

66 Arturo Toscanini (1867-1957).

67 Amy March Beach (known professionally as Mrs. H.H.A. Beach) was dubbed the "Dean of American Women Composers" by *Étude* magazine.

68 Rees is the only female composer to have written a national anthem. However, Rees' Transvaal anthem has since been superseded by the South African anthem.

69 After escaping several attempts on their lives, Alessandro Stradella (1642-1682) and his singing pupil, Hortensia (or, Ortensia), were both stabbed to death in their bedroom by hired assassins.

70 Pedrell helped to regenerate the music of Spain, and he was assisted by his three greatest students, Issac Albéniz (1860-1909), Enrique Granados (1867-1916), and Manuel de Falla (1876-1946). [Joaquim Turina (1882-1949) was also an important figure, for having used Spanish folk elements in his compositions.]

71 William Grant Still (1895-1978) broke strong racial barriers and became the first Afro-American to conduct in the deep South.

72 Matches: a matches *3*, b matches *4*, c matches *1*, and d matches *2*.

73   The composer is Walter (now Wendy) Carlos.

74   Anton "Ruby" Rubinstein (1821-1894).

75   The infant whose life was saved by his mother's escape to the belfry was Guiseppe Verdi.

76   Swedish composer, Johann Helmich Roman (1694-1758).

77   Niccolo Paganini.

POSTLUDE

BIBLIOGRAPHY

Many resources were used, to varying extents, in the compilation of this book, and they are listed here.

Abdul, Raoul. *Blacks in Classical Music.* New York: Dodd, Mead & Company, 1977.

Anderson, James. *The Complete Dictionary of Opera & Operetta.* New York: Wings Books, 1993.

Arvey, Verna. *In One Lifetime.* Fayetteville, AR: University of Arkansas Press, 1984.

Beach, Scott. *Musicdotes.* Berkeley, CA: Ten Speed Press, 1977.

Borge, Victor, and Robert Sherman. *My Favorite Comedies in Music.* New York: Franklin Watts, 1980.

Carter, Roy. *A Classical Music Quiz with Richard Baker.* North Pomfret, VT: David & Charles Inc., 1980.

Cohn, Arthur. *Musical Quizzical.* New York: MCA Music, 1970.

Cott, Ted. *The Victor Book of Musical Fun.* New York: Simon and Schuster, 1945.

Crafton, Ian, and Donald Fraser. *A Dictionary of Musical Quotations.* New York: Schirmer Books, 1985.

Crowest, Frederick James. *Musicians' Wit, Humour, And*

Anecdote. London, 1902; rpt. Ann Arbor, Michigan: Gryphon Books, 1971.

Dearling, Robert and Celia, with Brian Rust. *The Guinness Book of Music*, 2nd edition. Enfield, England: Guinness Superlatives Ltd., 1981.

Edwards, Arthur C. and Marrocco, W. Thomas. *Music in the United States*. Dubuque, IA: Wm. C. Brown Company Publishers, 1968.

Esar, Evan. *20,000 Quips & Quotes*. New York: Barnes & Noble Books, 1968.

Ewen, David. *American Composers: A Biographical Dictionary*. New York: G. P. Putnam's Sons, 1982.

Ewen, David and Slonimsky, Nicolas. *Fun with Musical Games and Quizzes*. New York: Prentice-Hall, Inc., 1952.

Finck, Henry T. *Musical Laughs*. New York: Funk & Wagnalls Company, 1924; rpt. Detroit, MI: Singing Tree Press-Book Tower, 1971.

Griffin, Clive D. *Classical Music*. Music Matters Series. London: Dryad Press Ltd, 1988.

Griffith, Benjamin W. *Who, What, When, Where, Why— In the World of Music and Art*. Hauppauge, New York: Barron's Educational Series, Inc., 1991.

Harris, Kenn. *The Ultimate Opera Quiz Book*. New York: Penquin Books, 1982.

Harvey, Edmund H., ed. *Reader's Digest Book of Facts*.

Pleasantville, New York: The Reader's Digest Association, Inc., 1987.

Humphrey, Laning. *The Humor of Music and Other Oddities in the Art.* Boston, MA: Crescendo Publishing Co., 1971.

Hurd, Michael. *The Orchestra.* New York: Facts on File, Inc., 1980.

Jablonski, Edward. *Encyclopedia of American Music.* Garden City, NY: Doubleday & Company, Inc., 1981.

Kamien, Roger. *Music: An Appreciation.* New York: McGraw-Hill Book Company, 1980.

Kaufmann, Helen L. *Anecdotes of Music and Musicians.* New York: Grosset & Dunlap, 1960.

Kreismer, Jack. *The Bathroom Trivia Book.* Saddle River, New Jersey: Red-Letter Press, Inc., 1986.

Kupferberg, Herbert. *The Book of Classical Music Lists.* New York: Facts on File Publications, 1985.

Lebrecht, Norman. *The Book of Musical Anecdotes.* New York: The Free Press, 1985.

Milligan, Harold V. and Souvaine, Geraldine, ed. *The Opera Quiz Book.* New York: A. A. Wyn, 1948.

Osborne, Charles, ed. *The Dictionary of Composers.* New York: Barnes & Noble Books, Inc., 1995.

Sadie, Stanley, ed. *The New Grove Dictionary of Music*

and Musicians. London: Macmillan Publishers Ltd., 1980.

Schmadel, Lutz D. *Dictionary of Minor Planet Names*. Berlin, Germany: Springer-Verlag, 1993.

Slonimsky, Nicolas. *A Thing or Two About Music*. Westport, CT: Greenwood Press, 1948.

Slonimsky, Nicolas. *Lectionary of Music*. New York: Doubleday, 1990.

Slonimsky, Nicolas. *Lexicon of Musical Invective*. Seattle, WA: University of Washington Press, 1965.

Still, Judith Anne, ed. *William Grant Still and the Fusion of Cultures in American Music,* 2nd edition. Flagstaff, AZ: The Master-Player Library, 1995.

Tripp, Rhoda Thomas. *The International Thesaurus of Quotations*. New York: Thomas Y. Cromwell Publishers, 1970.

Trivial Pursuit: Genius III Boardgame. Beverly, MA: Parker Brothers, 1994.

Westrup, J. A. and Harrison, F.Ll. *The New College Encyclopedia of Music*. William Collins Sons & Co. Ltd., 1976.

Young, Mark C., ed. *The Guinness Book of World Records: 1997,* Stamford, CT: Guinness Publishing Ltd., 1997.

OTHER GREAT RESOURCES

Here are a few more books that you will surely enjoy:

Borge, Victor, and Robert Sherman. *My Favorite Intermissions*. Garden City, NY: Doubleday & Company, 1971.

Gates, W. Francis. *Anecdotes of Great Musicians*. Philadelphia, PA: Theodore Presser Co., 1895; rpt. Philadephia, PA: Theodore Presser Co., 1923.

Levant, Oscar. *A Smattering of Ignorance*. Garden City, NY: Doubleday & Company Inc., 1939.

Ray, Robin. *Words on Music*. London, England: Methuen London Ltd., 1984.

Taylor, Deems. *Of Men and Music*. New York: Simon and Schuster, 1937.

Zahler, Diane and Zahler, Kathy A. *Test Your Cultural Literacy*. New York: Simon and Schuster, Inc., 1988.

ABOUT THE AUTHOR

LISA M. HUFFMAN

She is the granddaughter of composer-conductor William Grant Still (1895-1978) and pianist-journalist Verna Arvey (1910-1987). She received a Bachelor of Arts degree in Communications from the University of the Pacific, and she currently serves as Special Projects Coordinator for William Grant Still Music. Formerly, Lisa Huffman worked as Training Specialist for Pacific Mutual Life Insurance Company in Newport Beach, California.

ABOUT THE
CONSULTANT TO THE AUTHOR

DR. CAROLYN L. QUIN

Dr. Quin teaches Harmony, Class Piano, and Music Appreciation at Riverside Community College in Riverside, California. Formerly, she was Chair of the Department of Music at Winthrop University (South Carolina). She has been an Associate Professor of Music and Chair of the Division of Liberal Studies at Lane College (Tennessee), and the Executive Director of the Jackson (TN) Symphony Orchestra. Dr. Quin is a harpsichordist and frequent performer of chamber music. She has served as co-chair of the Chamber Music Panel and as a member of the Overview Panel for the National Endowment for the Arts. Dr. Quin received her Ph.D. at the University of Kentucky with a dissertation on Fanny Mendelssohn Hensel, and her Master of Music degree at the University of Arkansas. An active researcher and presenter of papers on Afro-American music for the last twelve years, Dr. Quin coauthored *William Grant Still: A Bio-Bibliography*, with Judith Anne Still and Michael Dabrishus (Greenwood Press, 1996).

ACKNOWLEDGMENTS

Special thanks to those individuals who research and write prolifically of their passions for classical music, for they have enabled me to put this book together. They, along with all classical music patrons, preserve a resonant part of all of our lives.

My special thanks also to:

Carolyn L. Quin, Ph.D., for the meticulous and conscientious consultation she provided to the author.

Victor Cano, artist, for the delightful illustrations found throughout this publication.

Lance Bowling of Cambria Master Recordings and to Michael Shott, Professor Emeritus at Northern Arizona, University in Flagstaff, Arizona for assistance in locating particularly helpful resources and for offering their own extensive classical music knowledge.

New Vision Technologies Inc. for permission to use clipart from their *Presentation Taskforce* software – g-clef (pages 9-21), harp (pages 63-76), piano (pages 89-102), conductor's stand (pages 115-133), and book (page 161); see also back cover.

T/Maker Company for the use of clipart from their *Clickart* software – bow tie (front cover) and eighth notes (pages 33-48); see also front and back covers.

Cover Design: Lisa M. Huffman

DO YOU KNOW ANY
CLASSICAL MUSIC TRIVIA
YOU WOULD LIKE TO SHARE?

If you have any trivia that you would like to share, we would love to hear about it for upcoming editions of *Classical Music Trivia*! Please write down your contribution and mail it to The Master-Player Library:

Trivia Contribution: (Attach extra pages if needed.)

_____

_____

_____

_____

_____

_____

_____

If available, please provide sources of information, i.e. book/article titles etc., for verifying your contribution.

Name:	_____
Address:	_____
City:	_____
State:	_____ Zip: _____

Mail to:
The Master-Player Library
P.O. Box 3044
Flagstaff, AZ 86003-3044

Need to order more copies of the
Classical Music Trivia book?

Please complete and mail in the following
information with payment of $6.95 plus $2.85
shipping and handling (per book):

Name: _____
Company: _____
Address: _____
_____
City: _____
State: _____ Zip: _____